DATE DUE	BORROWER'S NAME	ROOM NO.

Copyright © 2000 by NordSüd Verlag AG, Gossau Zürich, Switzerland
First published in Switzerland under the title *Wer fährt mit ans Meer?*
English translation copyright © 2000 by North-South Books Inc.
English translation by Rosemary Lanning.
Spanish translation © 2003 by North-South Books, Inc.
Spanish translation by Andrés Antreasyan.

First bilingual edition published in the United States and Canada in 2006 by
North-South Books, an imprint of NordSüd Verlag AG, Gossau Zürich, Switzerland.

First published in the United States, Great Britain, Canada,
Australia, and New Zealand in 2000 by North-South Books,
an imprint of NordSüd Verlag AG, Gossau Zürich, Switzerland.
Distributed in the United States by North-South Books Inc., New York.
Library of Congress Cataloging-in-Publication Data is available.
A CIP catalogue record for this book is available from The British Library.

ISBN-13: 978-0-7358-2037-1 / ISBN-10: 0-7358-2037-6 (trade edition) 10 9 8 7 6 5 4 3 2 1
ISBN-13: 978-0-7358-2038-8 / ISBN-10: 0-7358-2038-4 (paperback edition) 10 9 8 7 6 5 4 3 2 1

Printed in Germany

A MICHAEL NEUGEBAUER BOOK
NORTH-SOUTH BOOKS / NEW YORK / LONDON

How Will We Get to the Beach?

¿Cómo iremos a la playa?

BRIGITTE LUCIANI
ILLUSTRATED BY
EVE THARLET

One beautiful summer
day Roxanne decided to
go to the beach.
Everything she wanted to
take with her could be
counted on the fingers
of one hand:

**Una hermosa mañana de verano,
Rosana decide ir a la playa.
Todo lo que necesita llevar
se puede contar con los
dedos de una mano:**

the turtle,
the umbrella,
the thick book
of stories,
the ball, and,
of course, her baby.

**la tortuga,
la sombrilla,
el libro de cuentos,
la pelota y,
por supuesto, su bebé.**

But the car wouldn't start.

Pero el auto no arranca.

"Then we'll take the bus to the beach," said Roxanne.

—Entonces iremos a la playa en autobús —dice Rosana.

But something couldn't go
with them. What was it?

**Pero hay algo que no pueden
llevar. ¿Qué es?**

The little green turtle!

Animals weren't allowed on the bus.
"We can't go to the beach without the turtle!"
cried Roxanne.

¡La tortuguita verde!

En el autobús no se permiten animales.

**—No podemos ir a la playa sin la
tortuga —dice
Rosana suspirando.**

"Then we'll ride our bike to the beach," she said.

But something couldn't go with them. What was it?

—Entonces iremos a la playa en bicicleta —dice.

Pero hay algo que no pueden llevar. ¿Qué es?

The orange-spotted ball!

The ball wouldn't fit on the bicycle.
"We can't go to the beach without the ball!"
cried Roxanne.

La pelota de lunares naranja.

En la bicicleta no hay lugar para la pelota.

**—No podemos ir a la playa sin la pelota —dice
Rosana suspirando.**

"Then we'll ride our skateboard to the beach," she said.

But something couldn't go with them. What was it?

—Entonces iremos a la playa en patineta —dice.

Pero hay algo que no pueden llevar. ¿Qué es?

The big yellow umbrella.

Roxanne didn't have a free hand to hold it.
"We can't go to the beach without the umbrella!"
cried Roxanne.

La sombrilla amarilla.

Rosana no puede llevar la sombrilla en la mano.

**—No podemos ir a la playa sin la sombrilla —dice
Rosana suspirando.**

"Then we'll ride our kayak to the beach," she said.

But something couldn't go with them. What was it?

—Entonces iremos a la playa en kayak —dice.

Pero hay algo que no pueden llevar. ¿Qué es?

The thick blue book of stories.

The kayak was very wobbly, and the book might get wet.
"We can't go to the beach without the book!"
cried Roxanne.

El enorme libro de cuentos azul.

**El kayak se balancea demasiado
y el libro puede mojarse.**

**—No podemos ir a la playa sin el libro —dice
Rosana suspirando.**

"Then we'll fly in a balloon to the beach,"
she said.

But something couldn't go with them. What
was it?

**—Entonces iremos a la playa
en globo —dice.**

**Pero hay algo que no pueden llevar.
¿Qué es?**

Roxanne's baby!

He wouldn't climb aboard because he was
afraid of flying.
"We can't go to the beach without my baby!"
cried Roxanne. "He is more
important than all the other things.
I wouldn't go anywhere without my baby!"

Roxanne sighed. "How will we *ever* get to the beach?"

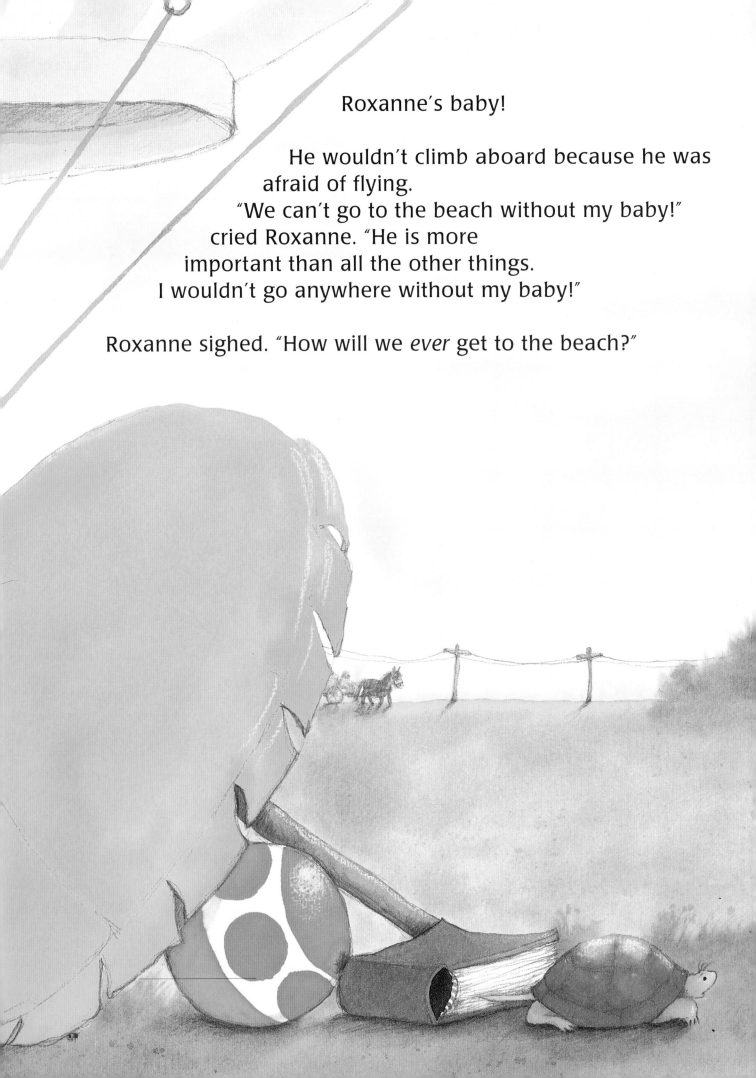

¡El bebé de Rosana!

El bebé no quiere subir al globo porque tiene miedo de volar.

—No podemos ir a la playa sin mi bebé —dice Rosana suspirando—. Él es lo más importante de todo. No iría a ningún lado sin mi bebé.

Rosana volvió a suspirar.

"Cómo iremos a la playa", se preguntó.

Just then a farmer passed by with his horse and cart.
He was on his way to the beach to sell cherries.

So they piled aboard: Roxanne, the green
turtle, the big yellow umbrella,
the thick blue book of stories,
the orange-spotted ball,
and, of course,
her baby.

En ese momento pasó un granjero con su carreta.
Iba camino a la playa a vender cerezas.

Y Rosana aprovechó para llevar todo:
la tortuga verde, la gran sombrilla
amarilla, el enorme libro de cuentos
azul, la pelota de lunares naranja
y, por supuesto, su bebé.

And they had a wonderful time!

¡Y todos pasaron un día maravilloso!